lauren child

whoops! But it wasn't Me

Grosset & Dunlap

Text based on script written by

Bridget Hurst and Carol Noble

Illustrations from the TV animation

produced by Tiger Aspect

GROSSET & DUNLAP
Published by the Penguin Group
Penguin Group (USA) Inc., 375 Hudson Street, New York, New York 10014, U.S.A.
Penguin Group (Canada), 90 Eglinton Avenue East, Suite 700, Toronto, Ontario, Canada M4P 2Y3
(a division of Pearson Penguin Canada Inc.)
Penguin Books Ltd, 80 Strand, London WC2R 0RL, England
Penguin Ireland, 25 St Stephen's Green, Dublin 2, Ireland
(a division of Penguin Books Ltd)
Penguin Group (Australia), 250 Camberwell Road, Camberwell, Victoria 3124, Australia
(a division of Pearson Australia Group Pty Ltd)
Penguin Books India Pvt Ltd, 11 Community Centre, Panchsheel Park, New Delhi - 110 017, India
Penguin Group (NZ), Cnr Airborne and Rosedale Roads, Albany, Auckland 1310, New Zealand
(a division of Pearson New Zealand Ltd)
Penguin Books (South Africa) (Pty) Ltd, 24 Sturdee Avenue, Rosebank, Johannesburg 2196, South Africa

Penguin Books Ltd, Registered Offices:
80 Strand, London WC2R 0RL, England

Library of Congress Control Number: 2006004506

ISBN 0-448-44413-5   10 9 8 7 6 5 4 3 2 1

I have this little sister, Lola.
She is small and very funny.
Sometimes Lola likes to play
with my things.
Usually I don't mind.

One day I come home from school
    with the best thing I have ever made.

Lola says, "Ooooh!"

I say,
"It took me ten days,
     three hours, and forty minutes
to make the outside,
          which is called
the superstructure . . .

" . . . It's built from three cereal boxes,

ten yogurt pots,

28
bottle
tops,

157
sweet
wrappers,
and a roll of
extra-wide
tinfoil...

two whole tubes of glue,
three pots of paint,
and half a roll of sticky tape."

Lola says, "Ooooh!"

I say, "Don't touch it!
This rocket is really breakable.
I don't mind you playing with
most of my things,
but you must double,
triple promise me
you will NEVER play
with this."

"Let's play something
        else then," says Lola.
    I say, "I've got to see Marv."
"But what am I going to do?" says Lola.
        And I say, "Why don't you play
with Soren Lorensen?"

Soren Lorensen is Lola's imaginary friend.
No one can see him except for Lola.

And Lola says,
    "Yes. Soren Lorensen always wants
to play with me."

"Hello, Soren Lorensen," says Lola.
"Charlie's gone to see Marv, so we can play
a very good game, can't we?"

And Soren Lorensen says,
    "Yes, with those two laughing
hyenas that are brothers and twins."

Lola says, "Yes, and Ellie,
    the tiny, small elephant.

"Where will the adventure be?"

Soren Lorensen says,
"In the place where all the **animals** live."

And Lola says,
"In a place a long way away."

"Oh no," says Soren Lorensen. "Ellie is really sad because he doesn't like the hyenas laughing at him and he's very far from home."

"Those **hyena** brother twins are **meanies**,
aren't they?" says Lola.
"What are we going to do?"

"We can't leave Ellie all **sad**," says Lola.
"He must go back to his nice friends in **elephant** land . . .
but how are we going to get him there?"

Then Soren Lorensen points to the rocket.

Lola says,
"But that is an extremely breakable and special rocket
and Charlie said that we should NOT ever
NEVER touch it or play with it."

"That's true," says Soren Lorensen, "but I think
what Charlie meant was that if we did play
with it, we must be extra specially
careful and not break it."

So Lola reaches up to get the rocket.

Soren Lorensen says,
    "Remember to be extra
specially careful, Lola."

And Lola says,

"I am!
I am being
extra specially
careful!"

Then she says,

"Whoops!"

Lola looks at the
pieces of broken rocket.
"You know, I think that
when things are broken
they can always be
mended together and made like new . . ."

"If we both act normally, Lola,
then Charlie will never know
we did it," says Soren Lorensen.

Lola whispers,

"No, he'll never know."

When I get home I shout,
"My rocket!
Lola!
Did you break
my rocket?"

Lola says,
"I didn't break your rocket, Charlie.
You absolutely told me to NOT
ever NEVER touch it . . . ever."

I say,
"You are telling a big lie, Lola!
And you know it!"

"Don't tell Mum!"
says Lola. "Wait, Charlie!
I just have to quickly talk
to Soren Lorensen."

Lola says, "Do you think we should tell Charlie
what really happened?"
Soren Lorensen says, "Maybe we should tell him
that somebody else broke the rocket?"
And Lola says, "Oh yes! Because it is nearly true!"

So Lola comes to talk to me.
"Charlie, Soren Lorensen and me have got something
very **extremely** important to tell you."

I say, "What?"

Lola says,
"It is the real **true** story of who **broke**
your special **rocket**."

"Well, me and Soren Lorensen were

playing in our room, Charlie,
and Ellie needed to go
in your **rocket**.

And I didn't think that
was a good idea,
but Ellie wouldn't listen.

So we all **squeezed** into the **rocket** so that we could go and find all Ellie's **nice** friends.

It was a real **squish**. But we did it.

"We took off. Higher and higher, right round the whole world. And then we went down and dow and · ★

down · ·
and
down

"... and when
we landed

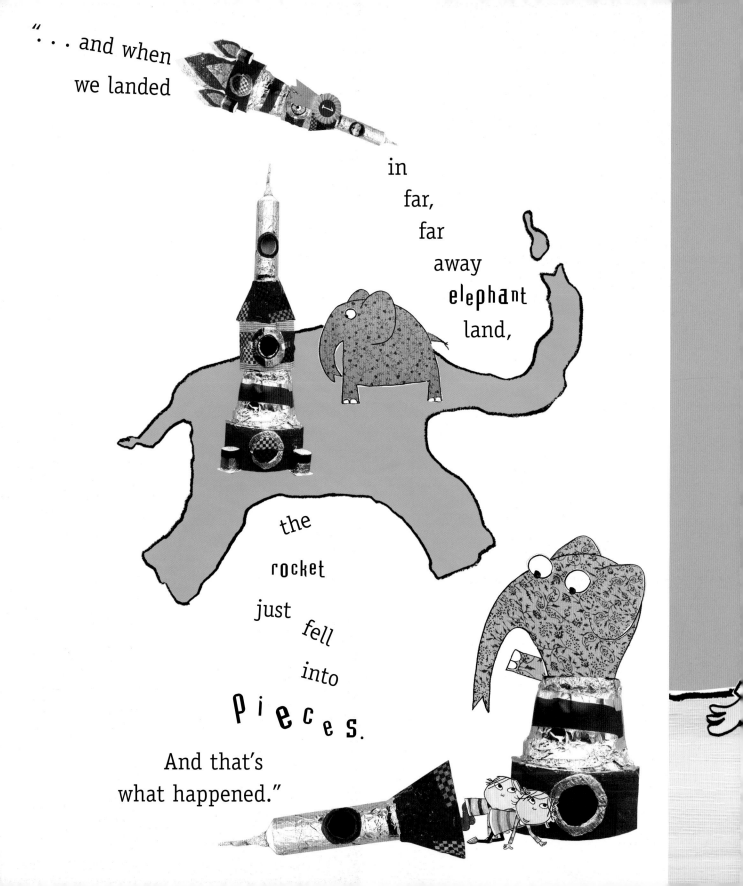

in
far,
far
away
e**l**e**p**h**a**n**t**
land,

the
rocket
just fell
into
P**i**e**c**e**s**.

And that's
what happened."

I say,
"Right.
I'm going
to tell
Mum."

"Oh dear, I don't think he **believed** us," says Soren Lorensen.

Lola says,
"I think I have to tell
Charlie the **truth**. But will it
make Charlie **like** me again?"

Soren Lorensen says,
"Yes, as long as you
say **sorry**, too."

Lola knocks at the door.
"Soren Lorensen
really wants to say sorry
for breaking your
rocket, Charlie."

So I just shut
the door.

Then there's another knock
and Lola says,
"It was me that broke
your rocket. I was playing
with Ellie and just as I was
getting your extremely
special rocket down from
the really high shelf . . .
it fell and broke
into lots
of pieces.

I am really
ever so very sorry
for breaking your
extremely special rocket,
Charlie."

And I say,
"Are you **really**, Lola?"

Lola says, "Really, **really**
truly **sorry**."
And she does look really very sorry.
So I say,
"That's okay. At least you've
told the **truth**."

Then Lola sees the rocket.

"You **mended** it, Charlie!" she says.

And I say,
"Yes, Lola, I've **mended** it."

"I like it," says Lola.
I say,

"Don't touch it!"